THE USBORNE GUIDE TO
e-mail

 Mark Wallace and Philippa Wingate

Designed by Neil Francis

Illustrated by Christyan Fox

Additional designs by Russell Punter

Cover design by Isaac Quaye

Technical consultants:
David Lee Taylor and
Richard Longhurst

*With thanks to Nicola Butler
and Gillian Doherty*

Contents

About this book

Electronic mail, or e-mail, is an amazing way to send messages from one computer to another. You can send a message to someone on the other side of the world and it will only take a couple of minutes to arrive. Ordinary mail is so slow by comparison that e-mail users call it "snail mail". E-mail is also cheap to use. Sending a message anywhere in the world only costs the price of a local telephone call.

E-mail is such a quick and efficient way of communicating that experts predict 450 million people will be using it by the year 2001. This book will make sure you are one of them.

Getting connected

E-mail is currently the most popular facility offered by a worldwide computer system called the Internet. This book tells you what the Internet is, and how it is used to send e-mail messages. On pages 8 and 9 you'll find out exactly what hardware and software you need to get connected to the Internet so you can use e-mail.

Features of e-mail

There's more to e-mail than just sending and receiving messages. On pages 24 and 25 you'll find out how to attach sounds, pictures, video clips and any other computer files to an e-mail. You can send a message to 20 people as quickly as sending it to just one person (see page 17).

Keeping track of your messages is simple too. E-mail programs automatically keep a copy of every message you send or receive. It's easy to organize these messages and store them in different places on your computer (see pages 18 and 19).

Most e-mail programs have many other useful features. For example, you can add a personal signature to all the messages you send or you can create an address book which makes it quicker to send messages to your friends (see pages 20 and 21). *The Usborne Guide to E-mail* helps you to use all these features and many others.

E-mail programs

There are lots of different programs you can use to send and receive e-mail. Most of the examples in this book use Microsoft® Outlook® Express (version 5), which is included with Microsoft® Windows® 95 and 98 operating systems. However, on pages 36 to 43 there is also a section that will show you how to use six other popular e-mail programs that are currently available.

Don't worry if the program you have is not covered or if you have a slightly different version of one of the programs included in the book. Most e-mail programs work in very similar ways. By following the instructions in this book, you should be able to figure out exactly how to use it.

Using this book

In this book, there are examples of how to use the different features an e-mail program offers. The examples are shown with numbered instructions and pictures, like the ones shown below. Each number on a picture indicates what you will see on your computer screen when you follow the matching instruction.

This example demonstrates how to attach a file to an e-mail message. (The full instructions for this are on page 24.)

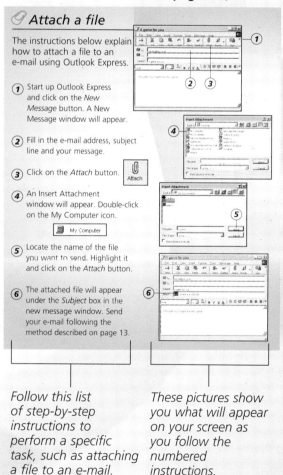

Attach a file

The instructions below explain how to attach a file to an e-mail using Outlook Express.

1. Start up Outlook Express and click on the *New Message* button. A New Message window will appear.

2. Fill in the e-mail address, subject line and your message.

3. Click on the *Attach* button.

4. An Insert Attachment window will appear. Double-click on the My Computer icon.

5. Locate the name of the file you want to send. Highlight it and click on the *Attach* button.

6. The attached file will appear under the *Subject* box in the new message window. Send your e-mail following the method described on page 13.

Follow this list of step-by-step instructions to perform a specific task, such as attaching a file to an e-mail.

These pictures show you what will appear on your screen as you follow the numbered instructions.

Life before e-mail

People have been finding different ways of sending each other messages for thousands of years. However, not all the methods they used were quite as quick or efficient as e-mail.

Hot news

Long ago, people used bonfires and smoke signals to send important messages. When England was threatened by the Spanish Armada in 1588, a chain of bonfires spread a warning from one end of the country to the other in only 18 minutes. However, fires were not a very reliable way of communicating if it was raining or foggy.

A Marathon effort

Messengers used to carry letters on foot or on horseback. In one famous incident in 490BC, a runner named Phidippides ran about 40km (just over 26 miles) to spread news of a Greek victory at the Battle of Marathon. Sadly, unlike today's long-distance runners, he hadn't done any training and died soon after from exhaustion.

Pigeon power

In Ancient Greece, messages were sent on small notes tied to the legs of trained homing-pigeons. Results from the Olympic games were sent from Athens to outlying towns in this way. A message could reach its destination within a few hours, unless the pigeons died or lost their way. When this happened, frustrated villagers were left with no idea who had won the javelin competition.

Getting organized

The first postal services started in China, Persia and the Roman Empire, and were all in operation by AD1. Messages were written on scrolls, and carried on horseback, or by ship. Because of the huge distances involved, messages could take weeks to arrive.

Ordinary citizens were not allowed to use the postal system, because it was reserved for government officials. However, most people didn't mind – they couldn't read or write anyway.

Mail for everyone

The first postal service that was open to the public was set up by King Louis XI of France in 1464. Mail was sent by messengers on horseback. Later, armed mail coaches were used to prevent robberies. In 18th-century England, letters were stolen so often that people began to cut bank notes in two and send each half separately.

During the 19th century, mail was sent by train, making the postal service much cheaper to use. The first air mail service began in 1918, between Washington, DC, and New York. Letters and packages could travel between the cities in just two days.

Messages by wire

The electric telegraph was invented in 1837. Messages could be sent huge distances very quickly. Telegraph machines spelled out words in morse code – a code in which combinations of dots and dashes made up each letter.

In 1866, a telegraph cable was laid under the Atlantic linking Europe and America. A telegraph message could travel between the continents in a few minutes, whereas a letter sent by boat took 11 days.

Messages in an instant

In 1863 an Italian priest sent a drawing over a wire – the first fax. His experiment took place about 120 years before the first fax machine was launched in 1984.

The first e-mail messages were sent in 1971, and in the 1980s messages were exchanged between computers in offices and universities that had been linked together. By 1990, e-mail had gone worldwide and beyond...

How e-mail works

E-mail is a way of sending messages from one computer to another. For this to work, the computers have to be linked together.

This section will explain how computers are linked and how e-mail messages are sent.

A group of computers that have been linked together is called a network.

What is a network?

A network is a group of computers that have been linked together. For example, the computers in a university might be linked so the students and researchers can share information.

Some companies with offices in different countries have large networks that link their computers all over the world.

The computers in a network normally exchange information through a central computer, called a server, which is connected by cables to each of them.

What is the Internet?

The Internet, or Net, is a huge network that links together millions of smaller networks. Telephone lines and cables connect networks all over the world to form the Net. This means it's possible to send an e-mail from Peru to Italy, or China to Denmark via the Net.

The networks that make up the Net are linked to powerful computers called routers. Messages sent via the Net travel from one router to another to reach their destination.

This diagram shows how an e-mail message can be sent across the world via the Internet.

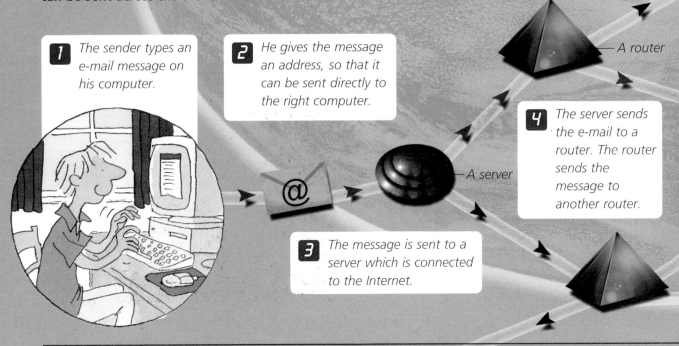

1 *The sender types an e-mail message on his computer.*

2 *He gives the message an address, so that it can be sent directly to the right computer.*

3 *The message is sent to a server which is connected to the Internet.*

4 *The server sends the e-mail to a router. The router sends the message to another router.*

A router

A server

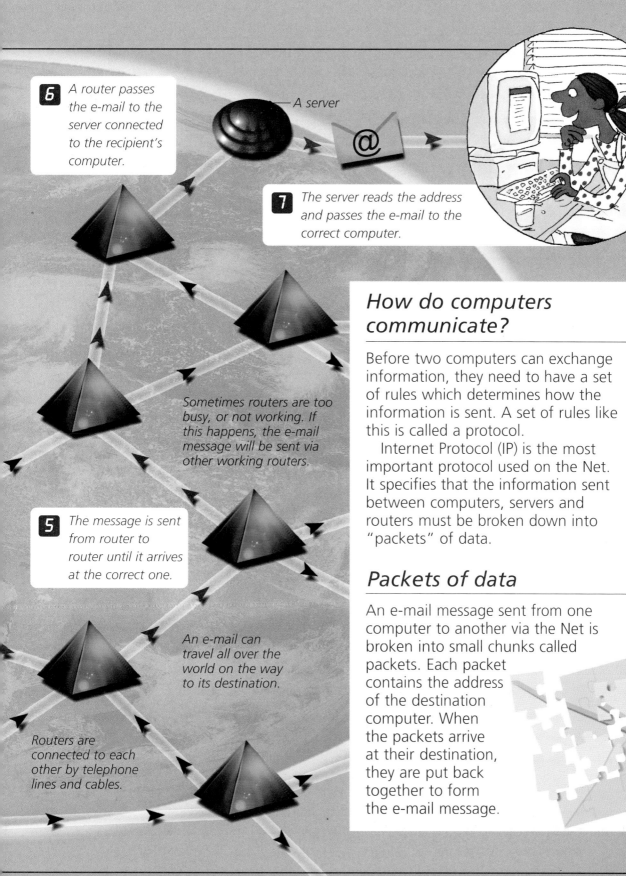

6 A router passes the e-mail to the server connected to the recipient's computer.

A server

7 The server reads the address and passes the e-mail to the correct computer.

Sometimes routers are too busy, or not working. If this happens, the e-mail message will be sent via other working routers.

5 The message is sent from router to router until it arrives at the correct one.

An e-mail can travel all over the world on the way to its destination.

Routers are connected to each other by telephone lines and cables.

How do computers communicate?

Before two computers can exchange information, they need to have a set of rules which determines how the information is sent. A set of rules like this is called a protocol.

Internet Protocol (IP) is the most important protocol used on the Net. It specifies that the information sent between computers, servers and routers must be broken down into "packets" of data.

Packets of data

An e-mail message sent from one computer to another via the Net is broken into small chunks called packets. Each packet contains the address of the destination computer. When the packets arrive at their destination, they are put back together to form the e-mail message.

Setting up your computer

To send and receive e-mail your computer needs to be online, which means connected to the Internet. This section tells you what hardware and software you will need to get connected.

What equipment do I need?

If you are using a computer in an office or school, you may find that it is already connected to a network which is linked to a server on the Internet. However, if you are using a computer at home, you'll need to connect it to a server via telephone lines. This is called a dial-up connection. The equipment you require to do this is listed below.

A computer

You don't need a really powerful computer to use e-mail. A PC needs at least a 486 processor chip; an Apple Macintosh needs a 3086 chip or better.

Your computer stores software on its hard disk. Space on a hard disk is measured in megabytes (MB). To store the software you need to use the Net, your computer must have at least 20MB of hard disk space free.

When it uses a program, your computer stores information in its memory. Space in a computer's memory is also measured in megabytes. To use Internet software, your computer needs to have at least 8MB of RAM (Random Access Memory).

A modem

An external modem

A modem is a device which enables computers to exchange information via telephone lines.

Computers produce data in the form of electrical pulses (called digital signals). Modems convert these signals into waves (called analog signals) that can travel along most telephone lines.

Two types of modems can be used with desktop computers: an internal modem which fits inside the computer, or an external modem, which is connected to the computer by a cable.

Modems transfer data to and from the Net at different speeds. The speed is measured in bits per second (bps). Ideally you should use a modem which works at 28,800bps or faster. The faster your modem works, the less time you'll spend waiting for e-mails to be transferred to and from your computer.

A telephone line

To connect to the Net, you'll need to connect your computer to your modem and your modem to a telephone line. Instructions about how to do this should be provided with your modem.

A service provider

If your computer isn't already connected to a server on the Net, you'll need a company called an Internet service provider (ISP). ISPs own servers that are connected to the Net. Setting up an account means they will allow you to connect your computer to their servers via a telephone line.

There is some advice on how to choose an ISP on page 46.

Internet software

Once you have selected an ISP, they will provide you with all the software you need to use the Internet. This is usually supplied on a CD-ROM or floppy disks. The software should include instructions about how to install it, which means put it on your computer's hard disk.

Getting started

Once you have finished installing the Internet software supplied by your ISP, your computer should automatically restart itself. A program will open which will guide you through a signing-in procedure, which is the process of opening your ISP account.

You will be asked to type in information such as your name and address. The details vary depending on which ISP you have chosen. When you have completed this information, your computer should connect itself to the Internet, or go online.

Passwords and user names

With your Internet software, your ISP will probably have sent you a password and a user name (see page 10) which will allow you, and only you, to use your Internet connection. You will be asked to type in this information. As part of the signing-in process, you may also be asked if you want to choose a new user name (see page 11).

Once you have finished the signing-in process your computer is ready to use the Internet to send e-mail

An e-mail program

The software your ISP sends you will include an e-mail program. On your computer's desktop display there should be an icon that allows you to open the program. The icon may show a letter, an envelope or a mailbox. Double-click on it. A window similar to the one shown on page 12 may open. This is your e-mail program window. You will use this window to send and receive your e-mail messages.

Getting help

The instructions on this page describe the most common method of getting connected to the Net. However, for a number of reasons the procedure you will need to follow may be different. If you have any problems, your ISP should have a telephone helpline which you can call for advice.

Make sure you know how much you will be charged to use this helpline, as some companies charge a high rate (see page 46).

E-mail addresses

All e-mail users have their own, unique e-mail address. This ensures that messages are sent to the correct computers. Your ISP will either give you an address or allow you to choose one.

What does an address look like?

An e-mail address has two main sections: the user name and the domain name. The two sections are separated by an @ symbol, which means "at". Here is a typical address:

mark@usborne.co.uk

User name   "At"   Domain name

User name

The user name is often the name or nickname of the person who will receive the e-mail. A name can be used in different ways. If, for example, your name was David Rowe, your user name could be drowe, davidrowe, davidr, dave or David_Rowe (in the last example, the names are separated by a symbol called an underscore).

People whose e-mail is sent to the same server have e-mail addresses with the same domain name.

Domain name

A domain name is the name of the server to which the message will be sent. For home computer users, this is normally the name of your service provider's computer.

Part of a domain name is called the domain type. This tells you the kind of organization where the server is located, such as "gov" for a government organization, and "edu" or "ac" for a school. Some domain types are listed below.

Domain names of computers outside the U.S.A. often end in a country code. For example, the code for the United Kingdom is "uk", France is "fr" and Australia is "au".

Dots (.) separate the various parts of the domain name.

Domain types

com or co	– a commercial company
edu or ac	– an educational establishment
gov	– a government organization
net	– Internet companies
org	– an organization

john@home.org
maria@home.org
jo@home.org
bert@home.org
pip@home.org

Each person can have an e-mail address with their own user name.

Cool e-mail addresses

Here are some unusual or famous e-mail addresses:

Bill Gates
billg@microsoft.com

President of the U.S.A.
president@whitehouse.gov

Prime minister of Pakistan
primeminister@pak.gov.pk

Santa Claus
santa@northpole.com

What punctuation is used?

E-mail addresses never contain commas, spaces or brackets. However, they often have hyphens and underscores. Addresses can include capital (or upper case) letters.

Can I choose my address?

Service providers will normally let you choose a user name when you open an account with them. However, it has to be a name that hasn't already been chosen by anyone else. Therefore, ISPs sometimes recommend that you use a combination of letters and numbers. So if, for example, your name was David Rowe, you could try drowe16 or david16 (the number could be your birthday).

If you want to choose your entire e-mail address, you will need to pay to have a domain name allocated to you, or registered. To do this, you will need to contact a domain name registration company. Normally, you will have to pay a fee every year for your domain name.

Finding out e-mail addresses

Before you can send an e-mail, you need to know the address of the person you are sending it to. The easiest way to find out someone's e-mail address is to ask them.

Finding an e-pal

If you don't know anyone who uses e-mail, you could use the Internet to find an e-mail pen friend, or "e-pal". Look at the Friendfactory Web site at **http://www.friendfactory.co.uk** or Kids' Space Connection Web site at **http://www.ks-connection.org/penpal/penpal.html**. Page 44 explains what a Web site is, and how to look at one.

With the Kids' Space Connection Web site you can make friends all over the world.

Sending a message

This section describes how to send e-mail using a program called Microsoft® Outlook® Express. Don't worry if you don't have this program; other e-mail programs work in a very similar way. The instructions below are aimed at people who have a dial-up connection to an ISP (see page 8).

Getting started

Start up Microsoft Outlook Express using the instructions on page 9. You may be asked to type in your password and user name. A window similar to this one will appear.

At the bottom of the window there is a box beside the words *When Outlook Express starts, go directly to my Inbox*. Click in the box to make sure that a ☑ mark appears.

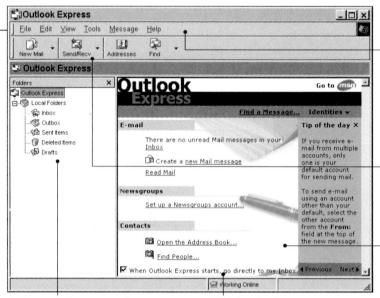

This area shows you how your messages are organized.

Click in the box beside this text.

The menu bar contains all the commands for the program.

The tool bar has the most important commands on it.

This frame helps you find the different parts of the program.

Writing a message

Every e-mail has three main parts: an e-mail address (see pages 10 and 11), a subject line and a message. The subject line is the first part of the message that is seen when it's received. Ideally, the person receiving an e-mail should be able to tell what it's about just by reading the subject line. So if, for example, you were arranging a meeting for lunch on Thursday, the subject line could be **Lunch on Thursday**.

The message itself can be any length. See page 14 and 15 for information about how to type your message into an e-mail message window.

Working offline

To save money by reducing the amount of time you spend online, you should write e-mails when you are offline (not connected to the Net). Then, when you have finished typing a message, you can go online to send it. To set up Outlook Express to work offline, start up the program, open the *File* menu and choose *Work Offline*.

Sending a message

The instructions below explain how to send an e-mail message using Outlook Express. To make sure that your e-mail is working, send a message to your own e-mail address to start with.

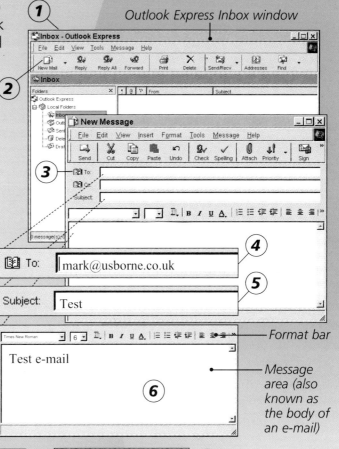

Outlook Express Inbox window

(1) Open the Outlook Express window as described on page 9.

(2) Click on the *New Mail* button.

New Mail

(3) A New Message window will appear.

(4) Click in the *To* box, and type in your own e-mail address.

mark@usborne.co.uk

(5) Click in the *Subject* box, and type **Test**.

Subject: Test

(6) Click in the message area, and type in the words **Test e-mail**.

Test e-mail

Format bar

Message area (also known as the body of an e-mail)

(7) Click on the *Send* button. A box will appear telling you the message is being sent to your Outbox. Click on the *OK* button.

Send

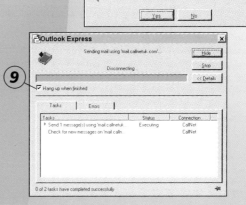

(8) Next, click on the *Send/Recv* button. When a box appears asking if you want to go online, click on the *Yes* button. You may be asked to type in your password and user name.

Send/Recv

(9) A box will appear telling you the message is being sent. To make sure your computer always disconnects after you have sent messages, click in the box next to *Hang up when finished* so that a ☑ mark appears.

Typing a message

This section explains how to use your keyboard to type a message into a new message window (see page 13).

You will also learn how to correct any mistakes you make as you type and change the appearance of the letters.

Finding keys on your keyboard

Letters, numbers and punctuation marks are known as characters. Most of the keys on a keyboard are for typing characters.

They are called character keys. The other keys on a keyboard are "control keys". Find out what some of them do below.

This picture shows you where to find some of the important control keys.

Backspace key – deletes the character to the left of the cursor.

Delete key – deletes the character to the right of the cursor.

Tab key – press to indent your text.

Shift key – press at the same time as a letter key to create a capital (upper case) letter.

Return key – to start a new line press once. To miss a line press twice.

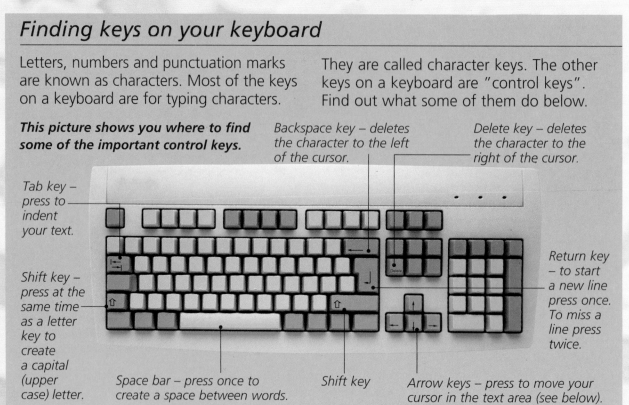

Space bar – press once to create a space between words.

Shift key

Arrow keys – press to move your cursor in the text area (see below).

Start typing an e-mail

Click in the message area of a new message window. A flashing line will appear. This is called your cursor. It indicates where any characters you type will appear. Type in your message.

Correcting mistakes

You can remove, or delete, any characters you type by mistake. Press the Delete key to remove the character to the right of your cursor, and the Backspace key to remove the character to the cursor's left.

Moving around

You can move your cursor around the part of the message area that contains text. This enables you to add or change any letters in your message.

You can move your cursor using the arrow keys. However, the quickest way to move it is with your mouse. As you move the pointer over your text, it changes into an I-shaped symbol. Place the pointer where you want the cursor to go, then click with your left mouse button. The cursor will jump to the place you clicked.

Selecting words

Once you have typed in your message, you can rearrange the words or change their appearance. To do this, you first need to indicate the words you want to alter. This process is called selecting.

To select some words, move your mouse pointer to the left of them, and press down your left mouse button. Keeping the button pressed down, drag your mouse across the words. The words that your mouse pointer passes over will be highlighted. Release your mouse button when your chosen words are highlighted.

To deselect the words, simply click on another part of the message area.

The first part of this text has been highlighted.

Dear Max, See you next week.

Moving and deleting text

To move a piece of text within the message area, you don't have to delete it and type it out again. Instead, you can move it using a technique called dragging and dropping

Select the word or phrase using the method described above, then click on the selected text and hold down your left mouse button. Drag your mouse pointer to a new position, then release the button. Your text will reappear in the new position. You can only drag and drop text within the part of the message area that contains text.

To delete a piece of text, simply select it and press the Delete key.

Making changes

Many e-mail programs allow you to change the style and size of the text you type in. To do this, you need to select the piece of text you want to alter. Then use the two boxes on the format bar (which appears above the message area of a new message window) in the way described below.

These two boxes are part of the format bar.

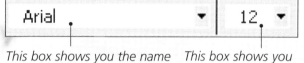

This box shows you the name of the current style of text. This box shows you the current letter size.

Changing font and size

A collection of letters in a certain style is known as a font. To change the font of a piece of text, select it and click on the arrow beside the font box. A list of choices will appear. To choose one, click on it.

The font list

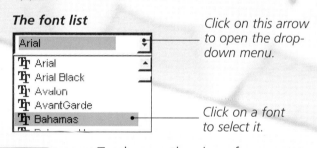

Click on this arrow to open the drop-down menu.

Click on a font to select it.

To change the size of your text, first select it. On the format bar, click on the arrow to the right of the text size box. Choose another size from the list.

Here are some actual text sizes.

size 10

size 12

size 18

size 24

size 30

Receiving a message

Any e-mails sent to you are kept by your ISP in a place called a mailbox. You will need to go online to move them from the mailbox to your computer. This is known as downloading your messages.

Receiving messages

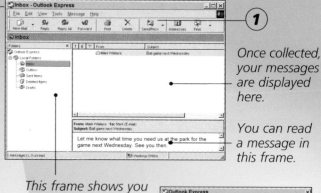

If you followed the instructions on page 13 and sent yourself an e-mail, you can now collect it. These instructions show you how to collect a message and print out a copy of it onto paper.

Once collected, your messages are displayed here.

You can read a message in this frame.

This frame shows you the folders where you can store mail (see pages 18 and 19).

(1) Open Outlook® Express. Click on the *Send/Recv* button. A box may appear asking if you want to go online. You will need to fill in your user name and password.

(2) A box will appear telling you that any messages in your Outbox are being sent, and that the computer is checking your mailbox for new messages. (You may see a different dialog box. It depends on your ISP.)

A message's subject line listed in the Inbox

(3) Any new mail will be downloaded into your Inbox. This can take a few minutes if there are lots of messages, or if any of them are very large. New messages will be listed in your Inbox.

Sender   *Subject*   *Date/time received*

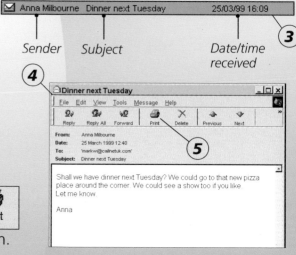

(4) To read a message, double-click on its subject line. A window will open containing the message.

(5) To print the message, make sure your printer is switched on and has paper in it. Click on the *Print* button.

Answering a message

There are two main ways of responding to an e-mail message: you can reply to it, or "forward it". E-mail makes it as quick and easy to send ten replies as it is to send one.

Replying

Replying to a message means sending an answer to the person who sent you the message. In most e-mail programs, you can reply to a message by clicking on a *Reply* button in the message window. In Microsoft Outlook Express it's called the *Reply to Sender* button. The e-mail program will create a new message window with the address and subject line filled in. The message area will contain the text of the original message. You can type in a reply and send it like any other message (see page 13). There are tips on how to edit the original message and compose a reply on page 23.

Reply to all

If you receive a message that has been sent to a group of people, you can send a reply to all the members of the group as well as the sender. In most e-mail programs, including Outlook Express, you click on the *Reply All* button, and then type in a reply in the usual way.

Forwarding

Sending an e-mail message you have received to another person or a group of people is called forwarding.

To forward a message, click on a *Forward* button in the message window. In Outlook Express it's called the *Forward* button. You'll see a new message window with the subject line and message filled in. Add the e-mail address of the person to whom you want to send the message, and then send it using the method described on page 13.

To send a message to lots of different people, just add extra addresses in the *Cc* (carbon copy) box which is under the *To* box. Separate each address with a semicolon (;). Most e-mail programs have a *Bcc* (blind carbon copy) box that lets you send the same message to several different people without them knowing who else has received it.

How long does it take?

Whether you are sending a message to India or to a friend next door, your e-mail should only take a couple of minutes, or even a few seconds, to arrive. If you send a message and it doesn't get returned to you, or "bounced back", within two minutes, you can be sure the message is safely on its way.

Organizing your messages

Imagine sending and receiving dozens of snail mail letters every day. It wouldn't be long before you lost track of which letters you had received, which you had read, which you had replied to and which ones you had thrown away. With e-mail, however, organizing your messages is simple.

Have I read this message?

It's easy to tell which of the messages listed in your Inbox you have read. All e-mail programs show the messages that you have read and the ones you haven't read in a different way.

In Microsoft® Outlook® Express, for example, all the messages listed in the Inbox have a little envelope symbol next to them. With unread messages, the envelope is yellow and closed. With read messages, the envelope is white and open. Unread messages may also appear in your Inbox in different text to the read messages.

A message listed in Outlook Express' Inbox before and after it has been read

| ✉ Philippa Wingate | New recipe | Fri 07/07/99 |

This message has not been read.

| ✉ Philippa Wingate | New recipe | Fri 07/07/99 |

This is the same message after it has been read.

I don't need this anymore

It's a good idea to get rid of any messages you don't need because they take up space on your computer's hard disk. E-mail programs make it very simple to delete messages. For example, to delete a message in Outlook Express, click on its subject line in your Inbox and click on the *Delete* button. The message will be stored in the Deleted Items folder.

✗ Delete

Outlook Express (version 5) can be instructed to delete any messages in its Deleted Items folder automatically when it is closed down. To choose this facility, click on the *Tools* menu and select *Options...* The Options box will appear. Click on the Maintenance tab and click in the box marked *Empty messages from the 'Deleted Items' folder on exit*. Then click on the *OK* button.

When you close the program a message will appear asking if you are sure that you want to delete the messages in the Deleted Items folder. If you do, click *Yes*. If not, click *No* and the messages will remain there.

Folders and mailboxes

An e-mail program can organize your messages by sorting them into places called folders. Your Inbox is a folder. In most e-mail programs folders are called mailboxes.

Your e-mail program will already have an Inbox which automatically receives new mail, an Outbox where your messages are kept before they are sent, a Sent Items folder containing a copy of every e-mail you send, and a Deleted Items folder which stores any unwanted messages.

You can create extra folders. For example, you may want to keep all your messages from one person in a single folder, or you could have a folder for any messages relating to a hobby or a sport you are interested in.

 ## Creating a new folder

These instructions explain how to create a new folder using Outlook Express

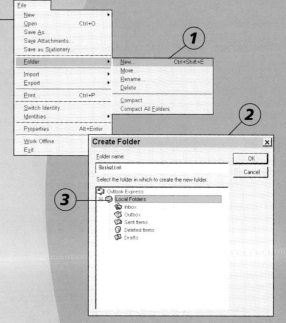

1. Open Outlook Express. The contents of your Inbox will be displayed in the window. Click on the *File* menu and select *Folder*. A submenu will open. Click on *New*.

2. A Create Folder window will appear. Type a name for your new folder, such as **Basketball**, in the *Folder name* box.

3. Click on the *Local Folders* icon in the window, and click on *OK*.

4. Your new folder will appear in the left-hand frame with the other folders.

5. To put a message into the folder, click on its subject line and, holding down the mouse button, drag it over to the new folder icon. Then release the mouse button.

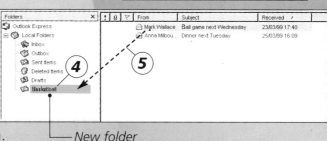

New folder

Personalize your e-mail program

Many e-mail programs include features which allow you to personalize the way in which they work. For example, you can add a signature to your e-mails, or create an address book containing a list of friends or business contacts.

E-mail signatures

To make your e-mails more personal, you can add a signature that will automatically appear at the end of every message you send.

An e-mail signature can only be made up of the letters and symbols on a keyboard. Some people use them to draw pictures, while others include jokes, or quotations from books or songs. For safety's sake, it's best not to include your home address or telephone number (see page 47).

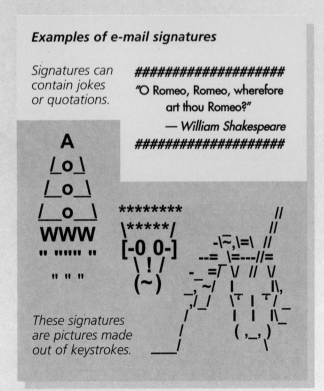

Examples of e-mail signatures

Signatures can contain jokes or quotations.

```
####################
"O Romeo, Romeo, wherefore
      art thou Romeo?"
        — William Shakespeare
####################
```

```
      A
    /_o_\
    /_o_\
   /__o__\
   WWW        *******       //
  " ...... "  \*****/       //
   " " "     [-0 0-]   -\~,\=\ //
             \ ! /    --= \=---//=
             (~)    -_ =Γ \/ // \/
                   _,~/ | _ I\,
                   _/_/ \Γ | Γ/
                   /      | | I\_
                  /       I \ I\_
                 /       ( ,_, )
               __/         \
```

These signatures are pictures made out of keystrokes.

Creating a signature

To create a signature in Outlook Express, select *Options...* in the *Tools* menu. In the Options dialog box, click on the Signatures tab. The Signatures sheet will appear. In the *Edit Signature* section, click in the *Text* box. Type in your signature. Then click on *Add signatures to all outgoing messages* and then click on the *OK* button.

Your signature will automatically appear in the message area when you create a new message. Simply delete it if you don't want to include it in a message.

The Outlook Express Options box

Click here to add a signature to your messages.

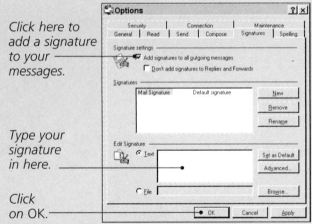

Type your signature in here.

Click on OK.

Tips

1 It's best not to make your signature more than six lines long. Some people find it annoying to get a message with a long signature.

2 If you want to include a picture, keep it simple. Complicated pictures do not always look right when a message is displayed in a different e-mail program from your own.

Address books

An address book of e-mail addresses enables you to send a message to someone without having to remember their e-mail address.

 ## *Use an address book*

These instructions show how to add a name to the address book in Microsoft Outlook Express and how to use the address book to send a message.

(1) Start up Outlook Express and click on the *Addresses* button.

(2) You'll see the Address Book window. Click on the *New* button and select *New Contact...* in the menu that appears.

(3) A Properties box will open. On the Name sheet, enter your contact's name and e-mail address. The name will appear in the *Display* box as you type.

(4) Click on *OK*. You'll see your new contact in the Address Book window. Close the window.

(5) To send a message to your contact, click on the *New Mail* button (see page 13). Double-click on the *To* button.

(6) A Select Recipients box will open. Double-click on your contact's name in the *Name* list, and then click on the *OK* button. Your message window's *To* box will now contain the contact's details.

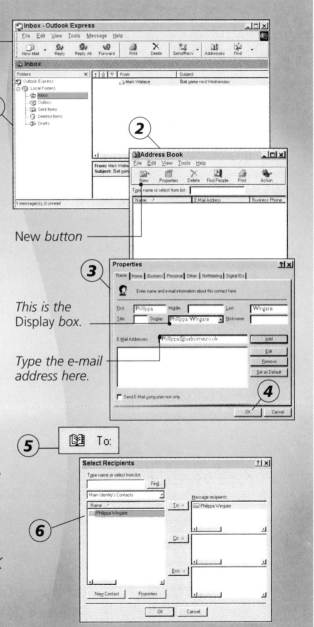

New *button*

This is the Display box.

Type the e-mail address here.

Writing good messages

E-mail is such a quick way of communicating that it's easy to be careless about the messages you send. This section will help you to write clear, polite messages that anyone will be happy to receive.

10 ways to write good messages

1 Give your message a subject line that conveys its content clearly. For example, **Can I borrow your book?** is better than **Book**.

2 Keep your messages simple and to-the-point. Think of your e-mail as a short note rather than a letter.

3 Don't send messages in capital letters. This is the e-mail equivalent of SHOUTING!

4 Check your spelling. It's easy to write messages very quickly and send them before you notice silly mistakes. Some e-mail programs have an option which will check your spelling. Alternatively, type an important message into a word processing program first. Check the spelling and then copy and paste it into a new e-mail message window.

5 Be careful if you are including funny comments. On the telephone it's easy to tell if someone's joking from their tone of voice, but people can easily misunderstand the tone of an e-mail. If in doubt, add a "smiley" (see page 29).

6 Don't use bold or italic letters, as most e-mail programs do not show them when they display a message.

7 Be careful what you write. E-mail is not always private and messages can accidentally be sent to the wrong person.

8 It's polite to reply to e-mails as soon as you can. With a letter, it's often acceptable to reply after a few days, but people may get annoyed if you don't respond to their e-mails within a day of receiving them.

9 When you receive a letter, you have time to think about your reply, write it, put a stamp on the envelope and put it in the mail. With e-mail it's easy to send a reply quickly and regret what you have typed. A rude or angry message is called a flame. Always consider your reply before you send it.

10 When you send a reply or forward a message, don't automatically include all of the original message. Try to edit it first (see the opposite page).

Editing messages

When you reply to, or forward, an e-mail (see page 17), the original message automatically appears in the new message window. It's a good idea to cut down, or edit, some of the text, removing anything that is irrelevant to your reply. If there are a number of points you want to respond to, you can insert your reply to each point individually as shown below.

This new message window shows the text of an original message before any editing has been done.

Click at the top of the message and type in your reply.

This text is called the header of the original e-mail message. To delete it, highlight it and press the Delete button on your keyboard.

You can delete any parts of the message that are not relevant to your reply.

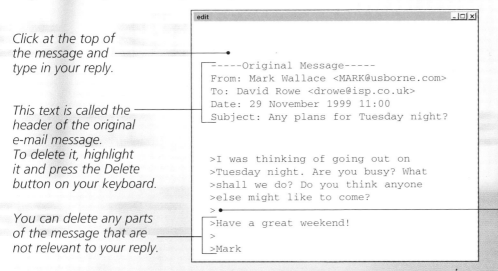

The > symbol is used in Outlook® Express to show which lines of the text belong to the original message. Different e-mail programs sometimes use other symbols.

After editing, your reply could look like this.

Your reply

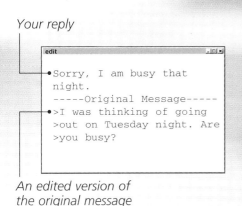

An edited version of the original message

This reply answers a number of points made in the original message.

Each answer can be inserted after the original question. Click at the point you want your text to appear, and then type in your answer.

Use the Return key to insert an extra line space.

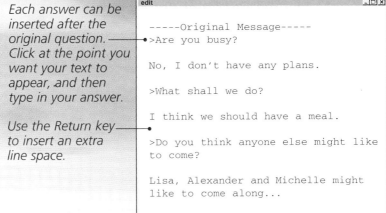

Attaching files to e-mails

You can send animated cartoons, pictures, sounds or even video clips by e-mail. In fact, anything that can be stored on your computer can, in theory, be sent by e-mail. A file sent this way is called an attachment.

This is part of an animated message that was designed to be sent by e-mail.

Programs, like this game, can be attached to an e-mail.

Attach a file

The instructions below explain how to attach a file to an e-mail using Outlook® Express.

1. Start up Outlook Express and click on the *New Message* button. A New Message window will appear.

2. Fill in the e-mail address, subject line and type in your message.

3. Click on the *Attach* button.

4. An Insert Attachment window will appear. Double-click on the My Computer icon.

5. Locate the name of the file you want to send. Select it and click on the *Attach* button.

6. The attached file will appear in an *Attach* box in the New Message window. Send your e-mail as normal.

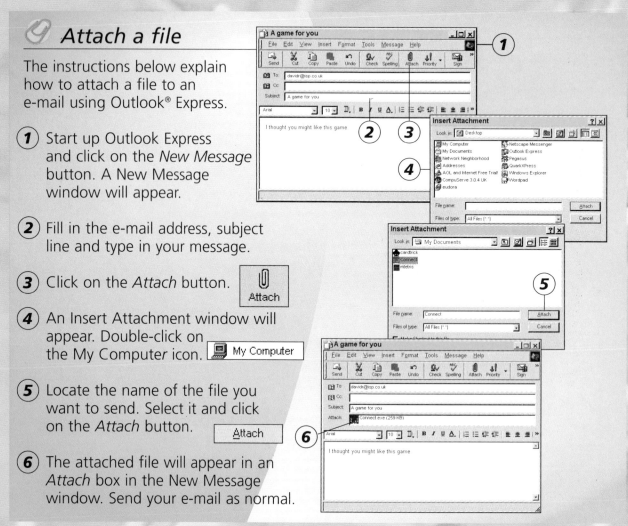

Receiving an attachment

When you receive an e-mail containing an attachment, the icon beside the message in your Inbox will look different. For example, Microsoft® e-mail programs display a paper clip.

First, you should make a copy of the attached file to store on your computer's hard disk. This will mean you won't have to open the e-mail every time you want to use the file. To do this in Outlook Express, open the e-mail message (see page 16). Click on the attachment's icon with your right mouse button and select *Save As...* from the menu that appears. In the Save As window, select a folder in which you would like to store the file, then click on the *Save* button.

Opening an attachment

Use the Windows Explorer or My Computer program (these are part of the Windows® 95 and 98 operating systems) to locate the folder in which you stored the attachment. Open the folder and double-click on the name of the attachment. The attachment will open.

Large files

If you want to send an attachment, make sure it is not too big to send. Files over 1MB in size can cause problems.

There are two problems with large attachments. First, if you are using a dial-up connection (see page 8), it will take several minutes to send or receive the message. Secondly, some ISPs will not transport messages that are over 1MB. So, if you want to send one, you need to make sure that your ISP will take large messages, and that the ISP of the person you're sending it to will accept it.

Some e-mail programs can break up a large message so you can send it in several sections. Alternatively you could compress the file into a smaller space, using a compression program such as WinZip (for PCs) or Stuffit (for Apple Macintosh).

Things to check when sending an attachment

1 Check what type of computer the person you are sending an attachment to is using. Certain types of files sent via e-mail from an Apple Macintosh to a PC, or vice versa, often will not work.

2 Make sure that the person who will receive your attachment has the right program to be able to use it. Some

files can only be viewed using a specific program. For example, picture files whose filenames end in **.TIF** can only be viewed using certain graphics programs.

3 If you use a compression program to compress a file (see above), the person receiving it will need the same program to decompress it.

Mailing lists

E-mail makes it possible to contact people all over the world who share the same interests as you. You can join a mailing list (also known as an e-mail list or e-mail group) which will send you regular e-mails about any subject you choose.

Types of mailing lists

Mailing lists fall into two main categories: announcement lists and chat lists. Announcement lists are usually run by an organization and are used to send out regular bulletins of information. If you join an announcement list you should only receive one or two e-mails from it each day.

Games

A chat list is like a discussion group. Members send e-mails to the list which are then forwarded to all the other members. For example, many sports teams have mailing lists where fans discuss recent matches. If you join a chat list, you could receive dozens of messages from it every day.

There are over 90,000 mailing lists available, covering almost any topic you can think of.

How can I find a mailing list?

The best way to find a mailing list you would like to join is to use the World Wide Web (see pages 44 and 45 to find out what the Web is and how to use it).

Two Web sites that have information about mailing lists are:
Liszt at **http://www.liszt.com** and PAML (Publicly Accessible Mailing Lists) at **http://www.neosoft.com/internet/paml**
Both sites allow you to search for mailing lists on specific subjects. On the Liszt site you can click on a subject category to see a page with mailing lists and subcategories. For example, if you click on the *Nature* category, you'll see a page showing subcategories including *Animals*, and mailing lists on subjects such as *Butterfly Photography*.

Science

When you join a list, e-mails from people all over the world who share your interests will be sent directly to your computer.

Sports

Wildlife

Joining a mailing list

Joining a mailing list is called subscribing. To subscribe to a list, you simply send an e-mail asking to join. Liszt and PAML's Web sites both tell you exactly what to put in your message, and the address to send it to, for each mailing list. There are some announcement lists that are run from Web sites. For example, a company called Merriam-Webster runs a "Word of the Day" list, which sends an e-mail to its members every day containing information about a particular word. You will find the Word of the Day list at **http://www.m-w.com/service/subinst.htm**.
    To join one of these lists, go to its Web site and follow the instructions listed there.

Music

Receiving e-mail from a list

Once you have subscribed to a list, you will initially be sent two e-mails. One is a welcome message telling you more about the list. This will include information about how to send messages to the list, and how to leave the list, or unsubscribe.
    The other message is automatically sent by the mailing list computer. You can delete this message.

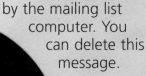

Food

Tips for using mailing lists

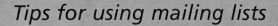

1 Only subscribe to one or two lists at a time, or you may end up receiving more e-mails than you can handle.

2 If a list sends out lots of messages every day, you can often ask to be sent a collection of messages, known as a digest, once a day or once a week.

3 Before writing to a mailing list, read the messages sent by the list for a week. You will learn how its members communicate, and will be able to avoid repeating points that have been made recently.

4 When you reply to a message, include part of the original e-mail (see page 23). This is called quoting. It helps list members identify the message you are responding to.

5 Don't reply to a message that is not appropriate to the discussion. It may be a troll – a message deliberately designed to annoy people.

6 Unsubscribe from your mailing lists if you are going away, and subscribe again when you get home, otherwise you may have hundreds of messages waiting for you.

Create your own mailing list

Whether you want to exchange gossip with a group of friends or discuss an interest so obscure that it isn't already covered by an existing list, you could start your own mailing list.

Small-scale mailing lists

A simple way to start a mailing list for a group of friends is to use your e-mail program. Type their addresses in the *To* box of a new message window, separating each address with a semicolon (;) or a comma (,).

To:	max@supernet.sa; maria@relenet.es; gretchen@worldwide.co.nz; mark@cyberside.edu; jeanpaul@verinet.co.fr

E-mail addresses separated with semicolons

Creating a group of contacts

Another way of setting up a small list is to use your address book to create a group of contacts. In Outlook® Express, click on the *Addresses* button. In the Address Book window, click on *New* and select *New Group*.

 The Outlook Express icon for a group

Give your mailing list a name in the *Group Name* box. If your friends are listed in your address book, click the *Select Members* button. If they are not, click the *New Contact* button and add their details to your address book first (see page 21). In the Select Group Members window double-click on the names of anyone you want to include in your mailing list. Then click *OK* to close the window and *OK* again. To send a message to your group, follow the method described on page 21 for using a contact.

Large-scale mailing lists

If you think your mailing list will attract lots of members, the best way to set it up is to use a Web site (see page 44). There are several sites which offer to administrate mailing lists (some of them are shown in the box on this page). They generally offer this service free of charge, but will often add advertising information to messages sent within the mailing list.

The Web sites allow you to choose what type of list you want to set up. You can create an announcement list, where only you can send messages to everyone on the list. Alternatively, you could set up a chat list. There are two main types of chat lists: a discussion list in which every message is sent to every member, or a moderated list in which every message is sent to you so that you can check it before sending it on to other members.

Helpful Web sites

The Web sites listed below include full instructions for how to set up your own mailing list.

eGroups at **http://www.egroups.com**

ListBot at **http://www.listbot.com**

ONElist at **http://www.onelist.com**

E-mail shorthand

E-mail has its own shorthand which will help you to make the tone and meaning of your messages easier to understand.

Smileys and emoticons

"Smileys", or "emoticons", are little pictures that help you to convey the emotion behind the words in an e-mail. They are made up of keyboard characters and when you look at them sideways they are like faces. You can insert one after a sentence to suggest its tone.

New smileys are being made up all the time. Here are just a few.

:-)	Happy	O:-)	Angel
:-D	Laughing	:-@	Screaming
:'-)	Crying with laughter	:-o	Wow!
:-(	Sad	:-&	Tongue-tied
:'-(	Very sad	I-O	Yawning
;-)	Winking	\o/	Hallelujah!
:*)	Clowning around	:-P	Tongue out
:^D	Great!	:*	Kissing

Acronyms

To avoid spending too much time typing, some e-mail users have taken to using acronyms, which are abbreviations of familiar phrases. They usually use the first letter of each word. Here are some of the most commonly used ones.

BTW	By The Way	**POV**	Point Of View
FYI	For Your Information	**OTOH**	On The Other Hand
IAE	In Any Event	**FC**	Fingers Crossed
IOW	In Other Words	**LOL**	Laughing Out Loud
TIA	Thanks In Advance	**NRN**	No Reply Necessary
IMHO	In My Humble Opinion	**ROFL**	Rolling On Floor Laughing

Unwanted e-mail

One annoying problem with snail mail is that you may receive junk mail from companies. E-mail is also used to send junk mail. Some businesses send messages advertising their products to thousands of users. Junk e-mail messages are known as spam mail.

Why do I receive spam mail?

When you receive spam mail the sender is likely to have found your e-mail address somewhere on the Net, or they may even have just guessed what it is.

Filters

One way of dealing with spam is to set up your e-mail program to get rid of messages that contain certain words or that are sent by certain people. This is called setting up a filter. A filter is an instruction that tells your e-mail program to put certain types of messages into specific places. For example, you could use a filter to send messages that contain the words "Free! Free! Free!" directly to your Deleted Items folder.

You can also use filters to organize messages. For example, a filter could instruct your e-mail program to place messages sent by a mailing list (see page 26) directly into a folder called Mailing List.

Kill files

A kill file is an instruction to your ISP's server to delete any messages sent to you by a specific person. Kill files are different from filters because they prevent unwelcome messages from ever reaching your computer.

This diagram shows the different ways you can instruct your computer to deal with unwanted e-mail.

A kill file will prevent certain messages from reaching your computer at all.

James

Maria

A filter can organize your mail into different folders.

Tom

Deleted Items

A filter can place unwanted messages straight into your Deleted Items folder.

Create a filter

These instructions explain how to create a filter that will delete messages sent to you by a certain person or organization. The filter will put unwanted mail into your Deleted Items folder.

(1) Start up Outlook® Express.

(2) Click on *Tools* and select *Message Rules* from the menu that appears. In the submenu that appears, select *Mail...*

(3) You'll see the New Mail Rule box. In section 1 of this box, click next to *Where the From line contains people.*

(4) In section 2 of the New Mail Rule box, click next to *Delete it.*

(5) In section 3 of the New Mail Rule box, click on *contains people.*

(6) In the Select People dialog box that appears, type in the e-mail address of the person or organization that is sending unwanted messages, and then click on the Add button.

(7) Click on *OK* in the Select People box and the New Mail Rule box to close them and return to your Inbox window.

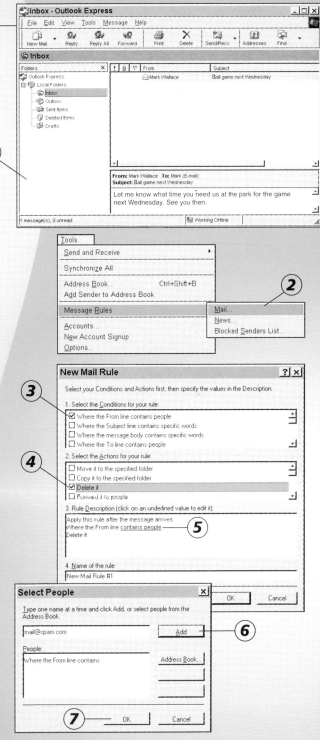

Going further

Some e-mail programs have extra features so you can do much more than just send and receive mail. They can help you to get yourself organized, or to use other parts of the Internet. Your e-mail program can even speak to you. Use the *Help* menu in your e-mail program to find out what special features it offers.

Automatic replies

Some e-mail programs can automatically reply to messages when you are away from your computer. In Microsoft Outlook, for example, this feature is called Out of Office Assistant. It's a useful way of letting people who urgently want to contact you know when you will be back.

Getting organized

E-mail programs sometimes include a range of features to help you get organized. They include, amongst other things, a calendar, an address book and to-do lists. Programs that help you to get organized are called personal information managers.

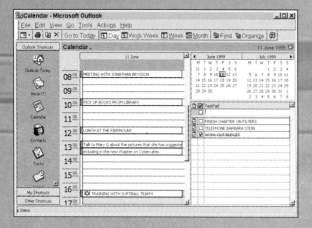

Microsoft Outlook 98 has a calendar to help you plan your day and remind you of events.

"You have new mail"

If your computer is permanently connected to the Internet, you may be able to instruct your e-mail program to display a message each time you receive new mail. This saves you from having to check for new e-mail from time to time.

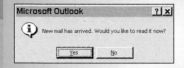

A message box will appear on your screen automatically.

Newsgroups

Newsgroups are Internet discussion groups where users can leave messages which other people can read and respond to. Some e-mail programs allow you to use newsgroups.

Newsgroups are quite like mailing lists (see pages 26 and 27). The main difference is that messages sent to a newsgroup are not automatically sent to all its members by e-mail. Instead, they are stored on a computer on the Net where anyone can read them.

Talking e-mail

Your computer can even speak to you, if you have the right equipment. You need a talking e-mail program such as Listen2, which will read out your messages after they have been downloaded.

Most home computers are supplied with all the equipment you need to hear sounds.

Speaking to your computer

Certain programs, for example Dragon NaturallySpeaking, allow you to speak to your computer. This type of program is known as a speech recognition program. It allows you to dictate your e-mail messages, letters and other documents to your computer. When you use a speech recognition program for the first time, you will need to spend time "training" it to understand your voice.

To use speech recognition programs, you will need a microphone connected to your computer.

This woman is using a speech recognition program.

Privacy and security

If you want to buy things by e-mail, you'll need to ensure that personal details, such as your credit card number, can't be seen by anyone else. Although sending an e-mail is generally safer than making a telephone call or sending a letter, it is not completely secure. Messages can be sent to the wrong place.

You should also consider that if you use e-mail in a workplace, your employer is entitled to read all your messages.

Thieves are operating on the Internet.

One way to make an e-mail more secure is to encrypt it. This means using a secret key code to jumble up a message before you send it. A recipient with a matching key will be able to unjumble or decrypt the message and read it. Many e-mail programs can be set up to encrypt messages.

10 things that can go wrong

Just as snail mail letters can get lost or delivered to the wrong person, e-mail isn't one hundred per cent reliable. Problems can occur with your computer, your ISP, or other users' equipment. This section offers advice for when things go wrong.

1 I can't get connected to the Net

The most common reason that your computer can't connect to your ISP's server is that you're using the wrong user name or password (see page 9). Your user name should be the part of your e-mail address that goes before the @ symbol. Your password is "case sensitive", which means you must use capital (upper case) letters and lower case letters correctly.

2 I still can't get connected

Check that all the cables connecting your computer, your modem and your telephone line are plugged in properly.

If you have an external modem, make sure that it's switched on. Check that your modem is working properly (there should be instructions supplied with it to help you).

Check your password and user name, your connections, and your computer settings, before you contact your ISP for help.

3 I STILL can't get connected

Another problem could be the way in which your modem has been set up. Go to your *Start* menu and select *Settings*, and *Control Panel*. In the window that appears, double-click on *Modems*. In the Modems Properties box that appears, click on *Properties* button on the General property sheet. In the box that appears, make sure that the box marked *Only connect at this speed* does not have a mark in it.

If you still have problems connecting, contact your ISP's telephone helpline*.

HELP!

4 I've just lost my connection

Your computer may disconnect from the Net if your modem is using the same line as your telephone or fax machine, and you try to use one of these. Try disconnecting them when you go online.

5 My e-mail has been returned

Sometimes e-mail messages can't be delivered and are returned, or "bounced" back to you. If this happens, you will receive a message telling you what is wrong. If the message says something like *Message Undeliverable: User Unknown*, make sure the address you used is exactly right before you try to send the message again. Occasionally messages are bounced back because there are problems with servers and routers on the Net.

Helplines can be expensive to telephone (see page 46).

6 My messages take ages to arrive

E-mails don't always arrive within a few minutes. Some ISPs only send and receive mail on the Internet once an hour, so messages can take a few hours to arrive. If there's a technical problem with the sender's or recipient's server, messages can be delayed for days.

E-mails can take more time to arrive than they should.

7 Oops! I clicked on *Send*, but I want to stop the message from going.

If you are working offline you can simply open up your Outbox and delete the message. If your modem has already started dialling up a connection, you can probably stop the message by clicking on a *Cancel* button or something similar. If you are online when you press *Send*, sorry, there's nothing you can do to stop it.

8 My messages look strange

You may run into unexpected problems with your e-mail program. For example, messages you send or receive may arrive with the text a different length on each line. If this happens, try using the program's *Help* menu to find out what to do (try looking under *reply format* in the *Help* index).

9 I've had a "virus warning" message

You may receive messages warning you about computer viruses spread via e-mail (see page 47). There are lots of these messages circulating. The message might warn you that opening an e-mail with a title such as *Join the club* or *Good times* will infect your computer with a virus that will destroy all the data on your hard disk. Don't panic! These warnings are hoaxes. You can't get a virus just by opening an e-mail message, but you can get one by opening an attachment (see page 24) sent with an e-mail message.

When you get a hoax message, don't forward these messages to anyone else, as they can be very annoying to receive.

Your computer can't catch a virus by simply receiving an e-mail message.

10 I've received a message saying I could win big prizes

You may receive a message saying that you could win money or other prizes if you forward the message to lots of other people. These messages are hoaxes. Don't forward them to anyone else. Ignore them.

Microsoft Outlook

Microsoft® Outlook® is an e-mail program which is an expanded version of Outlook® Express. It has a variety of extra features, such as an address book, a calendar and a daily appointments list. You can buy Outlook on its own, or as part of a set of programs called Microsoft® Office.

Working offline

To work offline, select *Services...* in the *Tools* menu. In the box that appears, click on the Services tab. Select *Microsoft Exchange Server* and click on the *Properties* button. In the box that appears, click on the General tab. Click next to *Manually control connection state*, and *Work offline and use dial-up networking*. Finally, click on *OK* in each of the boxes to close them.

Microsoft Outlook's Inbox window

Click on this button to create a new message.

This is the shortcut bar. It is used to switch between the different features Outlook offers, such as a contacts list, a calendar or a daily "to do" list. To see this list select Outlook Bar in the View menu.

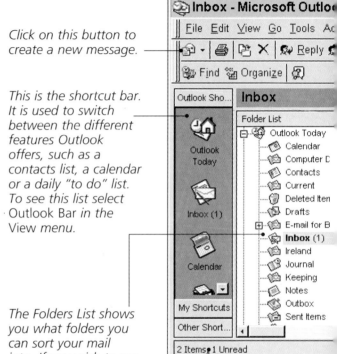

The Folders List shows you what folders you can sort your mail into. If you wish to see this list, select Folder List in the View menu.

This panel indicates how many messages are in the Inbox.

Sending and receiving messages

To create a new message, click on the *New Mail Message* button. A Message window, as shown below, will appear.

Fill in the Message window following the instructions on page 13. When you have completed your message, click on the *Send* button to transfer the message to your Outbox.

To send messages, click on the *Send and Receive* button. Your computer will go online, send your outgoing messages, and check for incoming ones. Any new messages will appear in your Inbox.

Send and Receive *button*

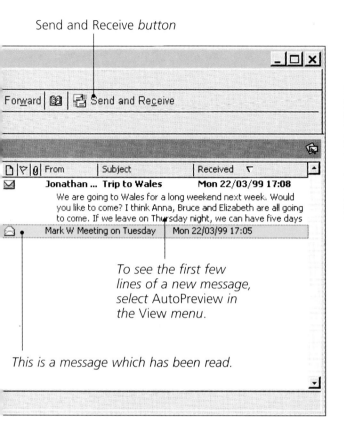

To see the first few lines of a new message, select AutoPreview *in the* View *menu.*

This is a message which has been read.

Creating a contact

Outlook has a list of contacts, as well as an address book. To create a contact, click on the *Contacts* icon on the Shortcut bar. A Contacts frame appears.

 Click on the *New Contact* button on the toolbar. Fill in the form that appears, and then click on the *Save and Close* button.

Save and — Close *button*

To use a contact, click on the Contacts icon in the Shortcut bar. Select the name of the person to whom you want to send the message. Then click the *New Message to Contact* button.

Organizing messages

To create a new folder, open the *File* menu, select *New* and then *Folder...* In the Create New Folder box, give the folder a name, select where you want to keep it, and click on *OK*. In the window that appears, click the *Yes* button.

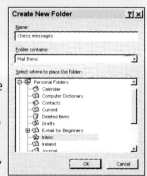

To move a message into a folder, select its subject line. Click on the *Move to Folder* button. In the menu that appears select *Move to Folder*. In the Move Items window select the name of the folder you require.

Extra features

Other features in Microsoft Outlook are included on the Shortcut bar. You can instruct the program to reply automatically to messages that are received while you are away. Use the *Out of Office Assistant* item on the *Tools* menu. There is a calendar that can be set to remind you of appointments, a "to do" list, and a system of notes you can use to write yourself reminders.

Send yourself a reminder like this one.

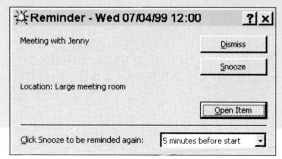

Pegasus Mail and Eudora Light

Pegasus Mail and Eudora Light® are free e-mail programs. They are often included on CD-ROMs attached to computer magazines.

Pegasus Mail

Experienced e-mail users like Pegasus Mail because it has a range of useful features including filters (see page 30).

 Working offline

To work offline, select *Enter offline mode* in the *File* menu.

 Sending and receiving messages

To create a new message, click on the *Start a new mail message* button.

Fill in the Message window that appears, and click on the *Send* button to transfer the message to your Outbox.

Click on the *Send and Receive* button to send your messages and check for incoming ones. Your computer will go online to do this.

Pegasus Mail's New mail folder

Reply button · Forward button · *Use the* Move *button to put a message into a folder.*

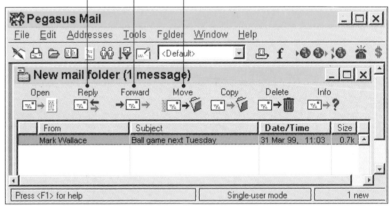

Address books

To create a new entry, click on the *Open or manage address books* button. In the window that appears, select the *New* button. Type a name for your address book in the *Long name for item box*, and click on *OK*. Select the name of your address book and click on the *Open* button. Click on the *Add* button and fill in the Edit address book entry form. Finally click *OK*.

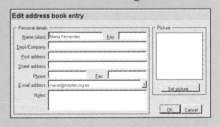

To use an entry double-click on a name in your address book.

Extra features

Pegasus Mail has a range of advanced features to filter your e-mails (see page 30). Use the *Help* menu to find out how to use them.

Eudora Light

Eudora Light is a very straightforward e-mail program. It displays all information in the main program window, using different frames instead of separate windows.

 Working offline

To work offline, select *Options...* in the *Tools* menu. In the *Category* section of the Options box click on *Getting Started*. Click on *Offline (no connections)* so that a mark appears in the box beside it. Then click *OK*.

 Sending and receiving messages

To create a new message, click on the *New Message* button.

A New Message frame will appear. Fill it in as on page 13. Click on the *Queue* button to transfer your message to the Outbox.

Queue

Click on the *Check Mail* button to send messages and check for new ones.

The Eudora Light Inbox

You can use the Redirect *button to send a message to someone else if it was sent to you by accident.*

Reply *button*

Forward *button*

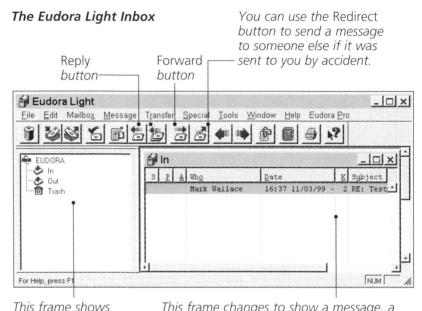

This frame shows your mailboxes.

This frame changes to show a message, a mailbox, your signature, or the address book.

 Address books

To create an entry, click on the *Address Book* button. An Address Book window will appear. Click on the *New* button. Type in a nickname for your contact and click on *OK*. Fill in the form that appears.

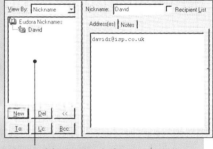

The Address Book frame

To use an entry, click on the *Address Book* button and double-click on a name in the list. This opens a New Message window.

 Extra features

When you create contacts in Eudora Light, you can give each one a nickname that will stand for the address. To send a message to a contact, you only have to type in their nickname. Use the *Help* menu to find out how to do this.

CompuServe Mail and AOL Mail

CompuServe and AOL are both companies with whom you can set up an account to use e-mail and the Internet. They provide their own e-mail programs as part of the Internet software they send to their new customers.

CompuServe Mail

CompuServe gives its customers a number instead of a user name. A number might be: **2345,4321**.

To use e-mail, start up the CompuServe program and click on the *Mail Centre* button. The screen shown on the right will appear.

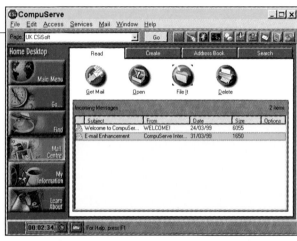

CompuServe's Mail Centre window

 Working offline

CompuServe will automatically work offline until you connect to send and receive your messages, as described below.

 Sending and receiving messages

To create a new message, click on the *Create* tab. On the screen which appears, click on the *New* button.

You'll see a Create Mail window. Fill it in as on page 13. Click on the *Send Later*

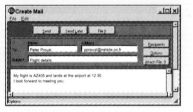

button to transfer your message to your Outbox.

In the *Mail* menu select *Send/Retrieve All Mail*. Your computer will go online, send your outgoing messages, and check for incoming ones. New messages will appear in your Inbox.

 Address books

To create an entry, click on the Address Book tab. Click on the *Add Entry* icon, and click on *OK* in the box

that appears. Fill in the details in the Define Address Book Entry box.

To use an entry, select

the person to whom you want to send a message in your address book, and then click on the *Create Mail Message* icon.

 Extra features

To send a message to another CompuServe user, you don't need their full e-mail address, just their user number. You will receive your user number when you sign up for the service.

AOL Mail

AOL Mail is popular because it is very simple to use.

 Working offline

To work offline, open the *Mail Room* menu and select *Set up Auto AOL (Flashsessions)*. A window will appear which will guide you through the process of working offline. Click on the *Walk Me Through* button.

 Sending and receiving messages

To create a new message, click on the *Write* button.

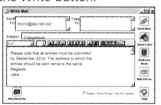

A Write Mail window will appear. Fill it in. Click on the *Send Later* button to transfer it to your Outbox. In the window that appears click on *OK*.

Click on the *Mail Room* button and select *Run Auto AOL (Flashsessions) Now*. Then click on *Begin*. Your computer will go online, send your out-going messages, and check for incoming ones.

To open a window that will show your folders, select Personal Filing Cabinet *in the* File *menu.*

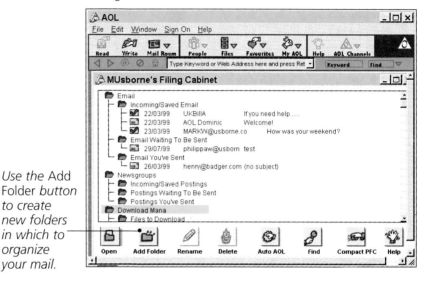

Use the Add Folder *button to create new folders in which to organize your mail.*

 **Address books**

To create an entry, click on the *Mail Room* button and select *Address Book* from the menu that appears. In the Address Book window, click on the *New Person* button. Fill in the New Person form and click on *OK*.

To use an entry, click on the *Address Book* button. Select the person to whom you want to send a message and click on the *Send To* button. Click on *OK* in the Address Book window to close it.

 Extra features

To view the Incoming/Saved Email window offline, click on the *Mail Room* button and select *Read Email Offline*. In the menu which appears, select *Incoming/Saved Email*.

Netscape Messenger

Netscape® Messenger is part of a set of programs called Netscape® Communicator. This also includes Netscape Navigator®, which is a popular browser (see page 44). The browser and e-mail programs are designed to be used together, so if you use Netscape Navigator to browse the World Wide Web, you may want to use Netscape Messenger for e-mail.

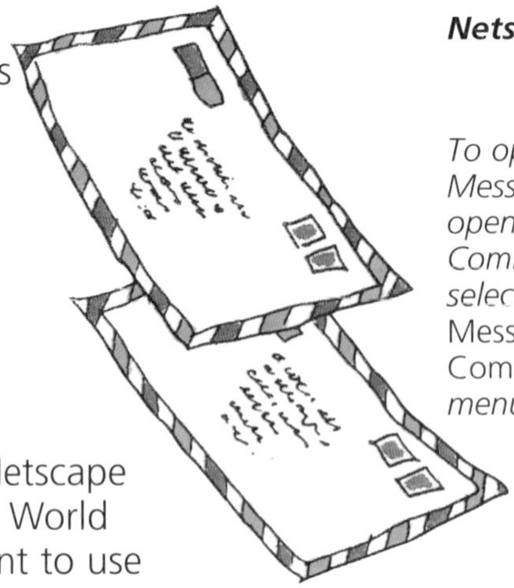

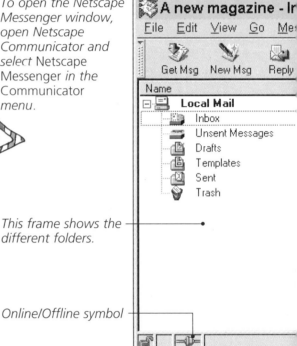

(see page 44)

Netscape Messenger's Inbox

To open the Netscape Messenger window, open Netscape Communicator and select Netscape Messenger *in the* Communicator *menu.*

This frame shows the different folders.

Online/Offline symbol

 ## Working offline

Look at the connection symbol at the bottom of the main Netscape Messenger window. If you see the online symbol, click on it to disconnect from the Internet.

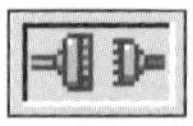

Offline

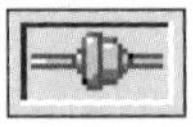

Online

 ## Sending and receiving messages

To create a new message, click on the *New Msg* button. A Composition window like the one below will appear . Fill it in as on page 13.

New Msg

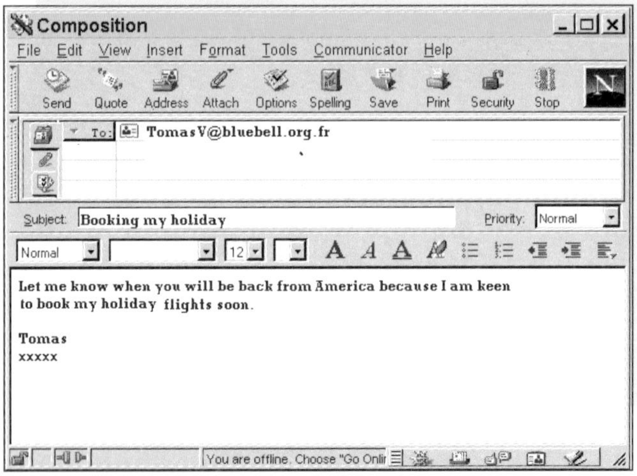

When you have completed your message, click on the *Send* button to transfer the message to your Outbox.

Send

When you are ready to send your message, click on the *Get Msg* button. Next, click on *Yes* in the window that appears asking if you want to go online. A window will appear asking you whether you want to send the messages in your Outbox. Click on *Yes* and enter your password. Your computer will go online, send your outgoing messages, and check for incoming ones.

Get Msg

Fill it in as on page 13.

This frame shows incoming messages. Double-click on the message line to see the whole message.

When you click on a message line, its contents is shown in this frame.

Organizing messages

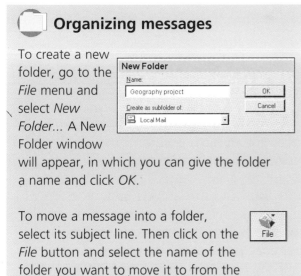

To create a new folder, go to the *File* menu and select *New Folder...* A New Folder window will appear, in which you can give the folder a name and click *OK*.

To move a message into a folder, select its subject line. Then click on the *File* button and select the name of the folder you want to move it to from the menu that appears. Your file will be transferred automatically.

Address books

To create an entry, select *Address Book* in the *Communicator* menu.

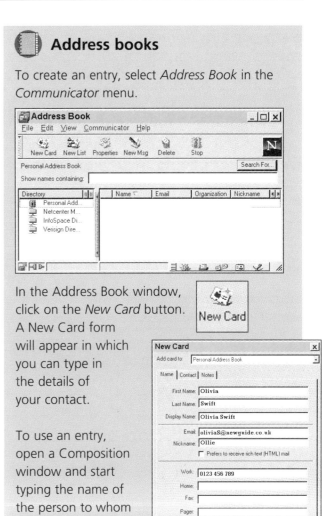

In the Address Book window, click on the *New Card* button. A New Card form will appear in which you can type in the details of your contact.

To use an entry, open a Composition window and start typing the name of the person to whom you wish to send a message. As you type, Netscape Messenger will complete the rest of the e-mail address for you. If it is the address you want, press Enter.

➕ Extra features

You can use the Communicator menu to switch over to other parts of the Netscape Communicator software, including its Web browser, Netscape Navigator.

Using the World Wide Web for e-mail

It is possible to send e-mail without having an e-mail program. You can use e-mail on a part of the Internet called the World Wide Web, or the Web. The big advantage of Web e-mail is that you can send and receive messages from any computer.

Wherever you are in the world, you can use Web e-mail to send or receive messages.

What is the World Wide Web?

The Web is made up of millions of documents called Web pages. These pages can include text, still and moving pictures, and sounds. A collection of Web pages that is created by a single organization or person is called a Web site.

Every Web page has its own address, called a URL (Uniform Resource Locator). This makes pages easy to find. A URL is similar to an e-mail address (see page 10). Here is a URL:

http://www.usborne.com/home.htm

This tells you that the page is a Web page.

This is the name of the computer on which the page is stored.

This tells the computer the filename of the Web page.

How do I use the Web?

To look at Web pages, you need to use a program called a browser. You will have one included with your Internet software (see page 9). Currently the most popular browsers are Microsoft® Internet Explorer and Netscape Navigator®. Internet Explorer is shown in the example below, but most programs work in a very similar way.

Microsoft Internet Explorer's browser window

Type a page's URL into your browser's Address box.

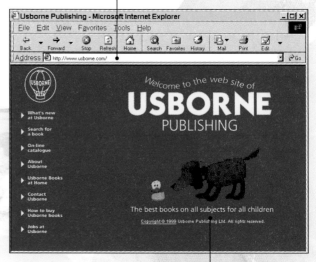

Web pages are displayed in this area.

To look at a Web page, open your browser program and make sure your computer is connected to the Internet. Type the URL of the Web page you want to look at in the *Address* box (this usually appears below the browser's tool bar). Press the Return key on your keyboard.

When your computer has located the page and transferred a copy of it onto your computer, it will appear in your browser's window.

Web e-mail services

Here are some Web sites that you can use to send and receive e-mails. They are free, and simple to use.

Hotmail at **http://www.hotmail.com**

Yahoo! Mail at **http://mail.yahoo.com**

MailExcite at **http://mail.excite.com**

Signing up for Web e-mail

To sign up for a Web e-mail service, go to the service's Web site by typing its URL into your browser. The exact method of signing up varies between different services, but each site contains a full set of instructions which explain exactly how to do it.

1. Create Your Yahoo! Email Name and Password
Yahoo! Mail Name: [_____] @yahoo.com
this will also be your Yahoo! ID (examples: **johnm** or **Joe_Bloggs** or **CoolDude56**)
Password [_____]
Re-enter Password [_____]
Password Question: [_____]
asked if you forget your password
(for example **What is my favorite pet's name?**)
Secret Answer: [_____]
required to retrieve your password

This is part of the form you fill out to sign up for the Yahoo! Mail service.

To move around from Web page to Web page when you are using the Web e-mail service's site, you need to click on hyperlinks. These usually appear as underlined words, often in blue. Your pointer will turn into a hand shape when it is positioned over a hyperlink. When you click on a hyperlink, your browser will automatically open another Web page for you.

Choosing a password

When you sign up with a Web e-mail service, you will need to choose a password. This will allow you to gain access to the mailbox where your messages are stored. It also prevents anyone else from reading your personal messages.

Make sure you choose a password you can remember.

err ··· what was it ···?

Using Web e-mail

To use your Web e-mail service, open your browser and type in the URL of the site. Enter your user name and password. Your own specially created page will appear. You can use it to send and receive messages.

A personal Web page on Yahoo! Mail

These underlined words are hyperlinks. Click on one to check for new messages or compose new ones.

One of the disadvantages of Web e-mail is that messages can take longer to arrive than those sent with an ordinary e-mail program.

Choosing an Internet service provider

An Internet service provider (ISP) is a company that gives you access to the Internet. Before you choose an ISP, it's important to find out about the services it offers.

This section tells you some of the questions to ask to make sure that you choose the ISP that will best suit your needs.

Finding an ISP

Ask friends who use the Net which ISPs they use and whether they would recommend them. Alternatively, buy an Internet magazine such as *Yahoo!*, *Wired* or *.net*. These contain advertisements for ISPs, detailing their services and telephone numbers.

Questions to ask

Once you have the name and number of an ISP that you are considering using, telephone the company and ask the following questions:

• Will they charge a fee to set up your account?

• Do they offer a free connection or is there a monthly fee charged? If there is a fee, does this include any free time online?

• Is there an extra charge for using the Net at peak times?

• Are there any other extra charges?

• Is there a free trial period? This is a useful period during which you can test out the services to make sure they meet your needs.

• Is the telephone number your modem will call to dial-up a connection charged at a local rate?

• How busy are the ISP's telephone lines? Will you be able to connect at the times that you want to? If you have the telephone numbers to which your modem will dial up, you could phone them at different times to see if they're busy.

• Will the ISP's telephone numbers work well with the modem you're using? If not, you might end up with a connection that transmits and receives data slowly.

• What e-mail program does the ISP provide? Is the software suitable for your computer?

• Will the ISP accept large e-mail messages and attachments (see page 25)?

What if things go wrong?

Even when your computer is set up and your e-mail software installed, you may still experience problems. Make sure your ISP has a telephone helpline providing technical support. If you are arranging a connection for your home computer, make sure the helpline is available in the evenings and on weekends when you are most likely to use the Internet.

Ask whether your ISP's technical support telephone helpline is charged at a local rate or is it more expensive? Many companies that do not charge you for Internet access, charge an expensive rate for using their helplines. You could try phoning the helpline to see whether it is easy to get through to, or whether it is often busy.

E-mail safety

E-mail enables you to contact, and be contacted by, people from all over the world. However, not everyone you come across via e-mail will have your best interests at heart. Here are some tips on how to stay safe when using e-mail.

 If you met a complete stranger in the street, you wouldn't give him your full name, home address and telephone number. So don't give this information to people you've contacted by e-mail. Remember, you don't know them.

 Never arrange to meet someone in person whom you've only corresponded with via e-mail. The people you meet this way are strangers, and may not be who they say they are.

 If you receive an e-mail containing anything you don't like, delete it immediately.

 Don't send a rude e-mail and think that it can't be traced back to you. It can. Every message that travels via e-mail contains information about the computer it came from, its route via the Internet, and its destination.

Writing rude e-mails could be bad for your health!

His head looks like a potato and he doesn't know....

Catching a virus

A computer virus is a program created to damage computer systems on purpose. Viruses can cause a variety of problems, from silly messages appearing on your screen, to the permanent destruction of information stored on your computer.

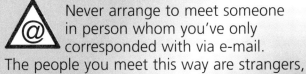

Viruses are "caught" by using infected programs on your computer. For example, an attachment (see page 25) sent to you via e-mail may contain a virus. When you use the program, the virus will infect your computer. A friend can send you an infected program without realizing. However, some people send viruses via e-mail on purpose. All you can do is be careful about which attachments you open.

How to avoid a virus

The best way to prevent viruses is to have virus-detection software installed on your computer. Use it to check any programs you receive via e-mail. You can buy this software at a computer store or obtain it from the Internet.

Always back up any important information on your computer regularly. This means copying the data onto floppy disks. Then, if your machine becomes infected by a virus, you can use your back-up disks to replace any information that is lost or damaged.

Index

Acknowledgments

Every effort has been made to trace the copyright holders of the material in this book. If any rights have been omitted, the publishers offer their sincere apologies and will rectify this in any subsequen editions following notification. Usborne Publishing Ltd. has taken every care to ensure that the instructions contained in this book are accurate and suitable for their intended purpose. However, they are not responsible for the content of, and do not sponsor, any Web site not owned by them, including those listed below, nor are they responsible for any exposure to offensive or inaccurate material which may appear on the Web site.

Screen shots reprinted by permission of Microsoft Corporation. Microsoft, the Microsoft logo, Microsoft® Internet Explorer, Microsoft® Outlook, Microsoft® Windows, Microsoft® Windows® 95 and Microsoft® Windows® 98, Microsoft Windows CE and Microsoft Window NT are either registered trademarks or trademarks of Microsoft Corproation in the US and other countries; cover – keyboard courtesy of Hewlett-Packard, p2 (also p6, 8, 16, 23, 30) Hewlett-Packard Pavilion Multimedia PC courtesy of Hewlett-Packard; p8 Telephone courtesy of British Telecommunications plc; Desktop modem – U.S. Robotics, Ltd; p11 Copyright © 1995-1999 Kids' Space™. All rights reserved; p14 Keyboard – Howard Allman; p24 Cupid program courtesy AdTools Inc.; Connect-It! courtesy Lazlo Safranyik, shareware author; p26 Pasta, guitar – Howard Allman; GP500 Motorcycle Racing game © 1999 Hasbro Interactive, Inc. © 1995-1999 Dorna; p33 DragonDictate voice recognition software courtesy Dragon Systems UK Ltd; p38 Pegasus Mail System, Copyright © 1990-99, David Harris, all rights reserved; p39 Eudora Light® is a registered trademark of QUALCOMM Incorporated; p40 Images kindly supplied by CompuServe; p 41 Images kindly supplied by AOL UK; p42 Netscape Communications Corporation has not authorized, sponsored, endorsed, or approved this publication and is not responsible for its content. Netscape and the Netscape Communications Corporate Logos, are trademarks and trade names of Netscape Communications Corporation. All other product names and/or logos are trademarks of their respective owners. Netscape, Netscape Certificater Server, Netscape FastTrack Server, Netscape Navigator®, Netscape ONE, SuiteSpot, and the Netscape N and Ship's Wheel logos are registered trademarks of Netscape Communications Corporation in the US and other countries; p44 Usborne Web site courtesy Usborne Publishing Ltd, www.usborne.com; p45 Yahoo! – Text and arwork copyright © by YAHOO! Inc. All rights reserved. YAHOO! and the YAHOO! logo are trademarks of YAHOO! Inc.